ILLUSTR8ED BY TOM LICHTENHELD

chronicle books · san francisco

Oh, and I just love your **2-2.**

They are **pre10**ding.

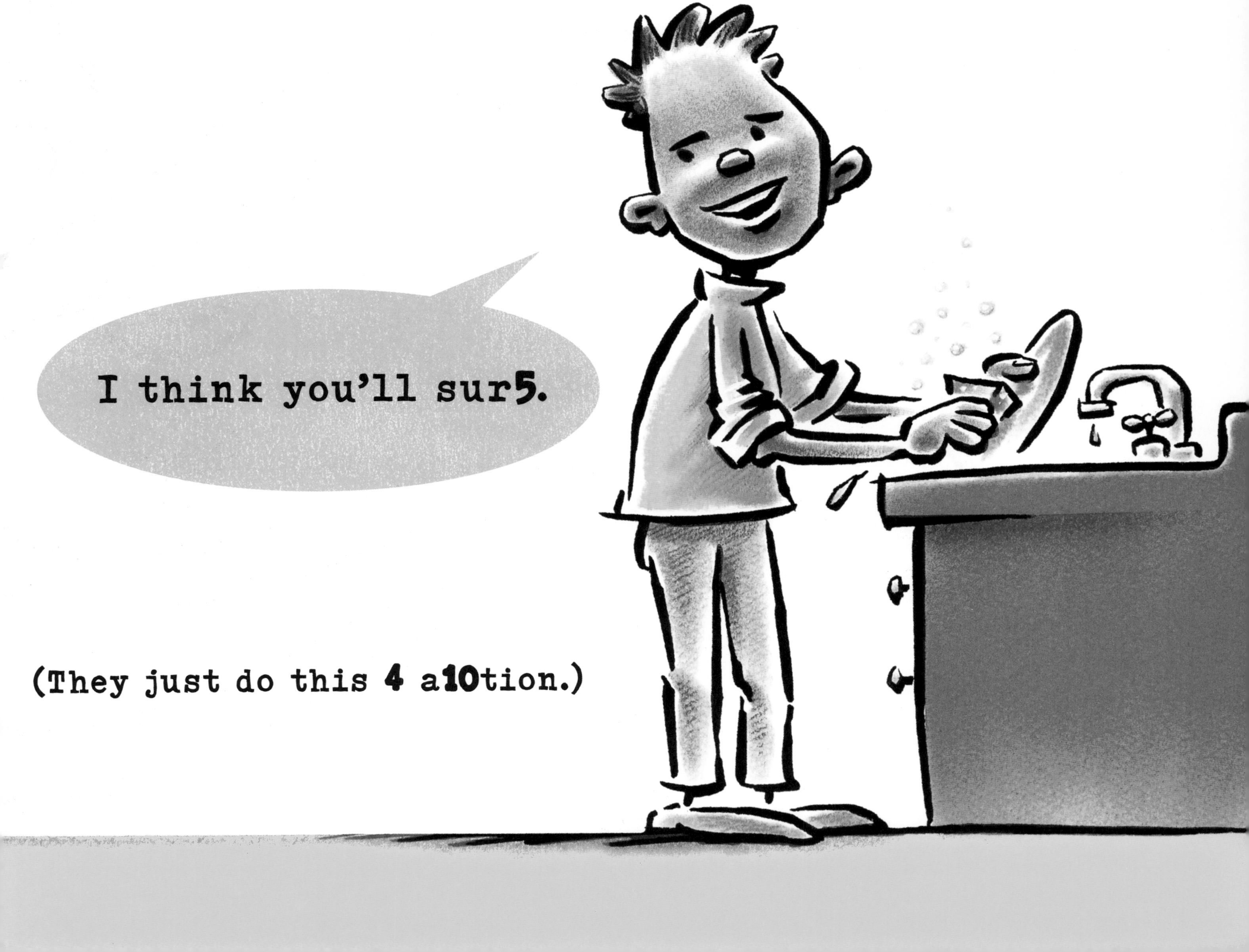

(They just do this 4 a10tion.)

Those sure are some orn8 **10**tacles.

Here's the plan: I'll climb the s2l and go str8 to the cookie jar. You be on the lookout 4 Mom.

Okay, but I'm frigh10d!

Wheeeeeeeeee! Flying **10**ies!

He lost his first **2**th!
He is el**8**ed!

it **10**ds **2** be a **4**mal affair.

I'm looking
4ward **2** a big piece
of cake!

They are in a **4**eign country.
Their **2**r guide is transl**8**ing.

C'est **4**midable, non?

It's gr**8**, right?

Pure con10tment.

A sh**80** spot **4** reading and writing.

We dedic8 this book 2
William Steig, the cr8or of *C D B!*
(cer10ly the inspiration
for this book) and so many
other cla6. —A.K.R. & T.L.

Library of Congress Cataloging-in-Publication Data available.

ISBN 978-1-4521-1022-6

Book design by Sara Gillingham. Typeset in ClickClack and Ultinoid.
The illustrations in this book were created with ink and PanPastels.

Manufactured in China.

FSC
www.fsc.org
MIX
Paper from responsible sources
FSC® C008047

1 3 5 7 9 10 8 6 4 2

Chronicle Books LLC
680 Second Street
San Francisco, California 94107

www.chroniclekids.com

Have you read Alice in 1derland?

Are you usually prompt, or do you 10d 2 be l8 and keep others w8ing?

What do you think you'll be like as 18ager?

What question would you ask a 4tune teller?